HENRY'S AWFUL MISTAKE

To librarians, parents, and teachers:

Henry's Awful Mistake is a Parents Magazine READ ALOUD Original — one title in a series of colorfully illustrated and fun-to-read stories that young readers will be sure to come back to time and time again.

Now, in this special school and library edition of *Henry's Awful Mistake,* adults have an even greater opportunity to increase children's responsiveness to reading and learning — and to have fun every step of the way.

When you finish this story, check the special section at the back of the book. There you will find games, projects, things to talk about, and other educational activities designed to make reading enjoyable by giving children and adults a chance to play together, work together, and talk over the story they have just read.

For a free color catalog describing Gareth Stevens' list of high-quality books, call 1-800-341-3569 (USA) or 1-800-461-9120 (Canada).

Parents Magazine READ ALOUD Originals:

Golly Gump Swallowed a Fly
The Housekeeper's Dog
Who Put the Pepper in the Pot?
Those Terrible Toy-Breakers
The Ghost in Dobbs Diner
The Biggest Shadow in the Zoo
The Old Man and the Afternoon Cat
Septimus Bean and His Amazing Machine
Sherlock Chick's First Case
A Garden for Miss Mouse
Witches Four
Bread and Honey

Pigs in the House
Milk and Cookies
But No Elephants
No Carrots for Harry!
Snow Lion
Henry's Awful Mistake
The Fox with Cold Feet
Get Well, Clown-Arounds!
Pets I Wouldn't Pick
Sherlock Chick and the Giant
 Egg Mystery

Library of Congress Cataloging-in-Publication Data

Quackenbush, Robert M.
    Henry's awful mistake / by Robert Quackenbush.
        p. cm. — (Parents Magazine read aloud original)
        Summary: Henry the duck tries all sorts of methods to rid his kitchen of an ant before his guest comes
to supper.
        ISBN 0-8368-0882-7
        [1. Ducks—Fiction. 2. Ants—Fiction. 3. Humorous stories.] I. Title. II. Series.
    PZ7.Q16He   1993
    [E]—dc20   92-32870

This North American library edition published in 1992 by Gareth Stevens
Publishing, 1555 North RiverCenter Drive, Suite 201, Milwaukee, Wisconsin
53212, USA, under an arrangement with Parents Magazine Press, New York.

Text © 1980 by Robert Quackenbush. End matter © 1992 by Gruner + Jahr, USA,
Publishing/Gareth Stevens, Inc.

Printed in the United States of America

1 2 3 4 5 6 7 8 9 98 97 96 95 94 93

HENRY'S AWFUL MISTAKE

by Robert Quackenbush

GARETH STEVENS PUBLISHING • MILWAUKEE
PARENTS MAGAZINE PRESS · NEW YORK

A Parents Magazine
Read Aloud Original.

For Piet
and his Grandma Q.
and Margie
and Leslie B.

The day Henry the Duck
asked his friend Clara
over for supper,
he found an ant
in the kitchen.

Henry was worried
that Clara
would see the ant.
She might think
his house was not clean.
The ant had to go.

Henry reached for
a can of ant spray.
But he didn't want
to spray near the food
he was cooking.
So he chased the ant
with a frying pan.

Henry ran around
the kitchen,
chasing after the ant.
But the ant got away
and hid behind the stove.

Henry took the food
he was cooking
off the stove.
Then he shut off the flame
and pulled the stove
away from the wall.
He saw the ant!

The ant saw Henry
and ran into
a small crack in the wall.
Henry went and got
a hammer.

Henry pounded a big
hole in the wall
where the crack was.
But he couldn't find the ant.
So he kept on pounding.

The hole got bigger
and bigger.
At last, Henry saw
the ant sitting
on a pipe inside
the wall.

Henry aimed the hammer
at the ant—and missed.
The blow of the hammer
broke the pipe.

Water came shooting
out of the pipe.
Henry couldn't stop it.

Henry grabbed a towel.
He tied it around the pipe
and the water stopped
shooting out.

But Henry hadn't stopped
the water soon enough.
It had sprayed
all over the kitchen.
Everything was soaking wet,
except for Clara's supper,
thank goodness.

Henry began mopping up
the puddles of water.
All at once, he slipped and
banged against the
kitchen table.
Everything came
crashing down.
Henry was covered with
pots and pans and food.

The supper was ruined.
There was nothing
Henry could do now
but to call Clara
and tell her not to come.

While Henry was
talking on the telephone,
the towel came loose
from the pipe.
The water came shooting out
and flooded the whole house.
Henry was carried right out
the front door by the flood.

There was no going back.
Poor Henry's house was
washed away by the flood.
He saved what he could
and moved into
a new house.

When Henry was settled
in his new house,
he again asked Clara
over for supper.
Just as he went to the door
to let Clara in,
he saw an ant.

He looked the other way!

Notes to Grown-ups

Major Themes

Here is a quick guide to the significant themes and concepts at work in *Henry's Awful Mistake:*

- The need to look ahead to the possible consequences of our actions
- Showing concern for a friend's opinion to the exclusion of all else can create problems

Step-by-step Ideas for Reading and Talking

Here are some ideas for further give-and-take between grown-ups and children. The following topics encourage creative discussion of *Henry's Awful Mistake* and invite the kind of open-ended response that is consistent with many contemporary approaches to reading, including Whole Language:

- Encourage your child to create a story about following an idea to its extreme. Ask your child to make up a silly ending to the story and a serious one.
- Can your child spot the ant in all except two of the pictures? Ask your child how Henry might feel if he saw the ant in the midst of all his troubles.
- What are the differences in the way we treat ants we see inside the house and outside the house? Some religions state that you should never kill any living creature, including insects. Ask your child if and how your family members differ in the way they treat different insects in the house. For example, does your child and your family react to spiders, often considered a helpful household insect, differently than centipedes? Why?
- Does your child like to cook? Ask him or her to describe a favorite meal. What part of the meal could your child help make?

Games for Learning

Children love to stir, shake, mash, and bake. In short, like Henry, they like to cook. In additon to learning how ingredients mix together, cooking activities give children's fine motor muscles (the muscles they use in writing) exercise and training. A child who can stir in a circle can make a letter *O* more easily. Here are some suggestions for cooking activities:

Cider Sauce

Your child can help you peel, slice and dice, and cut safely with a serated plastic knife.

In a large saucepan, heat until just boiling:

1/2 cup (125 ml) frozen apple juice concentrate
1/2 cup (125 ml) water seasoned with four whole cloves
1/4 teaspoon (1.25 ml) ginger
1/4 teaspoon (1.25 ml) cinnamon

Add 4 apples that you and your child have cored, sliced, and diced. Simmer until the apples are soft. Serve warm over ice cream.

Butter

Shaking cream into butter is a fun way to direct your child's pent-up energy on a rainy day. Just put whipping cream into a small glass jar with a tight-fitting lid, and take turns shaking it until you see the cream begin to thicken. Then keep shaking until it separates into butter and buttermilk. Pour off the milk and shake some more until all the buttermilk is shaken out. Drain a final time, salt lightly, spread on a cracker, and enjoy!